I SLIDE INTO THE WHITE OF WINTER

I SLIDE INTO THE WHITE OF WINTER

Charlotte Agell

Tilbury House, Publishers
Gardiner, Maine

To Phoebe,
and in memory of Douglas

Tilbury House, Publishers
132 Water Street
Gardiner, ME 04345

First Printing

Agell, Charlotte
    I slide into the white of Winter / Charlotte Agell.
        p.   cm.
    Summary: A family enjoys a day of hiking, sledding, and bellysliding in the snowy woods.
    ISBN 0-88448-115-8 : $7.95
    [1. Snow--Fiction. 2. Winter--Fiction. 3.Family life--Fiction.]
    I. Title.
    PZ2.A2665Iak   1994
    [E]--dc20
                                                                          94-4860
                                                                            CIP
                                                                            AC

Designed by Edith Allard and Charlotte Agell
Editing and production: Mark Melnicove, Lisa Reece,
Devon Phillips, and Lisa Holbrook
Office and warehouse: Jolene Collins

Imagesetting: High Resolution, Inc., Camden, Maine
Color separations: Graphic Color Service, Fairfield, Maine
Printing: Eusey Press, Leominster, Massachusetts
Binding: The Book Press, Brattleboro, Vermont

We walk
into the white of winter.

I am purple.

My friend is mostly green.

My brother is a rainbow
on mama's blue back.

We take the forest path,
the snow is deep in places.

We walk a long time.
There is nobody else.

I step in a drift
and pull my foot up with no boot!

It is silent in the woods
except for crows,
except for us!
We're laughing.

Mama says
bears might be asleep nearby.

We reach the hilly field.

We climb to the tip-top
and stop to catch our breath.

It comes out all steamy.
We are dragons in the winter!

Down we go. . .
whoosh!

Whoosh!

Mama calls,
    "Watch out for that . . .

tree!"

I tumble and crash,
the snow is soft.
My sled goes on without me.

The sky is only blue,
no clouds.

My cheeks sting,
my heart bumps-bumps in my ears.
I am okay.

We trudge up the hill together.

My brother keeps taking off his mitten
to eat snow. He cries
when his hand gets cold.

Mama takes a turn.

At the bottom of the field,
there is an icy patch.

The ice is nice
for bellysliding!

Far across the field
papa is coming to meet us!

We make a family of snow angels.

Snow gets up my shirt —
I am cold.

To warm up, we have hot chocolate
with only one cup.
And oranges.

We sit on our sleds,
and put the peel in our pockets.

Everyone is still hungry.
It is time to go home.